Dear Parent:
Your child's love of reading starts here!

Every child learns to read in a different way and at his or her own speed. Some go back and forth between reading levels and read favorite books again and again. Others read through each level in order. You can help your young reader improve and become more confident by encouraging his or her own interests and abilities. From books your child reads with you to the first books he or she reads alone, there are I Can Read Books for every stage of reading:

SHARED READING
Basic language, word repetition, and whimsical illustrations, ideal for sharing with your emergent reader

BEGINNING READING
Short sentences, familiar words, and simple concepts for children eager to read on their own

READING WITH HELP
Engaging stories, longer sentences, and language play for developing readers

READING ALONE
Complex plots, challenging vocabulary, and high-interest topics for the independent reader

ADVANCED READING
Short paragraphs, chapters, and exciting themes for the perfect bridge to chapter books

I Can Read Books have introduced children to the joy of reading since 1957. Featuring award-winning authors and illustrators and a fabulous cast of beloved characters, I Can Read Books set the standard for beginning readers.

A lifetime of discovery begins with the magical words "I Can Read!"

Visit www.icanread.com for information
on enriching your child's reading experience.

An Imprint of Sterling Publishing
387 Park Avenue South
New York, NY 10016

ADVENTURES OF MIA

ISBN 978-1-4351-5061-4

Manufactured in Dong Guan City, China
Lot #:
13 14 15 16 17 SCP 5 4 3 2 1
08/13

An I Can Read Book™

Adventures of Mia

Sandy Creek
NEW YORK

Adventures of Mia

Table of Contents

Mia
and the
Too Big Tutu

by Robin Farley
pictures by Aleksey and Olga Ivanov

Mia wishes to be just like her big sister.

A dancer!

Mom helps Mia's wish
come true.

It is time for class.

Mia is all set to go.

She does not forget a thing.

When Mom calls, "Ready?"
Mia grabs her bag.
She is ready!

Mia skips to school
with her bag in hand.
"Bye, Mom," calls Mia.
She does not want to be late.

Miss Bird's
SCHOOL of DANCE

"Welcome, dancers,"
sings Miss Bird.
Mia grins from ear to ear.

Mia hurries to change.
She wants to be first
on the dance floor.

Mia zips up her leotard.

She slips on her shoes.

She ties a ribbon in her hair.

Mia saves the best for last.
A pretty, pink, fluffy tutu!

The tutu is too big!

Mia packed her sister's tutu!

Mia pulls it up. It falls down.

She tugs it up.

It falls!

Mia hides.

Her heart sinks.

Mia is too bashful
to see Miss Bird now.

Mia spots her friend Ruby.

"My tutu is too big.

I'll trip!" she tells Ruby.

"My legs are too long,"
says Ruby.
"I always trip!"

The friends peek at the class.

Miss Bird is dancing sweetly.

"I like Miss Bird," says Ruby.

"I'll dance," says Mia,
"if you dance, too!"

Mia and Ruby tiptoe
onto the floor.
Mia's tutu slips. Ruby trips.

Miss Bird teaches a dance.
She spins. She leaps.
She walks on her toes!

"Who will try the dance?"
sings Miss Bird.
Nobody will try.

Miss Bird spots Mia and Ruby.
They are hiding in the back.
"Dance!" sings Miss Bird.

Mia and Ruby
are very brave.

They spin.

They leap.

They walk on their toes!

The class claps!

They cheer, too.

Mia forgets her
tutu is too big!
Mia and Ruby take a bow.

Dictionary

Leotard

(you say it like this: lee-o-tard)

The outfit that dancers wear

Pirouette

(you say it like this: pira-wet)

A very fast twirl

Tutu

(you say it like this: too-too)

A skirt that some dancers

wear over their leotards

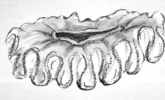

Mia
and the Dance for Two

by Robin Farley
pictures by Aleksey and Olga Ivanov

Today in class,
Mia is going to learn a dance
for two.

She is going to dance
with her best friend, Ruby!

Mia slips on her slippers.
She is ready to dance.

"Where is Ruby?"

Mia wonders.

She waits and waits.

Then Mia sees Ruby's mom.
She is talking to Miss Bird.

Ruby is sick.

Ruby will not dance today.

"All dancers
on the dance floor!"
sings Miss Bird.

Mia does not have
a partner for the dance
for two.

Mia feels very lonely.

Mia feels a tap, tap, tap.
"Will you be my partner?"
asks Bella.

Mia feels a pat, pat, pat.
"Will you be my partner?"
asks Ali.

Mia looks at Bella.

She looks at Ali.

Now Mia has too many
partners for the dance
for two!

Miss Bird starts class.

"One, two, three, four,"

she counts.

Mia knows how it feels
to be alone.

She does not want her
friends to feel lonely.

Mia's eyes sparkle.

She whispers to her teacher.

"A fine idea!"
sings Miss Bird.

"Will you be my partner?"
Mia asks Bella.

"Will you be my partner?"
Mia asks Ali.

Mia takes her friends
by the hands.

"Let's dance!" she tells them.

The friends spring
to their toes!

They twirl around
and around!

The three friends are happy
dancing the dance for two!

"Bravo!" sings Miss Bird.

Dictionary

First Position

Stand with your heels together and your toes pointed outward, forming a straight line.

Second Position

Stand with your toes pointed outward and your heels a foot apart.

Third Position

Stand with one foot in front of the other so the heel of the front foot touches the middle of the back foot.

Fourth Position

Start in Third Position and take a small step forward with your front foot.

Fifth Position

Stand with one foot in front of the other so the heel of each foot touches the toes of the other foot.

Mia
and the
Daisy Dance

by Robin Farley
pictures by Aleksey and Olga Ivanov

"Class," sings
Miss Bird.
"Good news!

The Daisy Dance is soon.

It is a big show!"

Mia jumps for joy!
Each dancer gets
to do a solo.

Mia will drop flowers,
and Anna will twirl
onstage!

Miss Bird teaches
the new dance.

But Anna does not dance.

She does not want to.

She wants to go home.

Mia is worried.

She wants the Daisy Dance
to go well.

Anna looks scared.

Mia wants to help.

But how?

At home, Mia practices
the new dance
over and over.

Mia hears
thump, thump, thump
on the door.

"Who is it?"

she asks.

"Will you help me
learn my steps?"
asks Anna.

"I have never done
a twirl," says Anna.
"Have you?"

Mia smiles.

Mia knows how it feels
to be scared.

"Yes!" says Mia.
"I will dance with you,
and we will both learn!"

Mia twirls and stops.

She hops and kicks.

Then she takes a big bow.

"Now you try,"
says Mia.
"You can do it!"

Mia and Anna dance
the steps over and over.

When it's time
for the Daisy Dance,
Anna is ready!

Mia drops flowers onstage.

Anna does a twirl.

All the dancers hop and kick.

The Daisy Dance is great!

Mia and Anna are happy.

They take a big bow.

Dictionary

Daisy

(you say it like this: day-zee)

A big white flower

Solo

(you say it like this:

sew-low)

A dance all on your own

Twirl

(you say it like

this: t-werl)

When a dancer

spins around

Mia
and the
Big Sister Ballet

by Robin Farley
pictures by Aleksey and Olga Ivanov

Mia is in the city!
Her dance class
is visiting the theater.

Mia's sister
will be there!

Mia's sister is named Ava.

Ava is a dancer!

Mia and her friends
watch Ava onstage.

Ava twirls and leaps.

She is a star!

The curtain closes.

Ava bows.

The class cheers!

Now Ava will show
the class a new dance!

Miss Bird takes the class
up to the stage.

Ava wears
blue toe shoes.
She has on a blue tutu.

"Let's dance!"

Ava says.

Mia watches Ava twirl.

Then Mia twirls.

Mia dances her best.

"Look, Ava!" she says.

But Ava is busy.

She is helping others.

Ava helps Anna point her toes.

Ava helps Ruby bend her legs
into a plié.

Ava helps Bella spring
into the air.

And Ava helps Tess spin
around and around.

But Ava doesn't help Mia.

And Ava doesn't see
Mia dance her best.

Mia is sad.
She sits down
on a bench.

She doesn't feel
like dancing anymore.

Ava sees Mia.
"Why don't you
want to dance?"
Ava asks.

"You were too busy
to watch me," Mia tells her.

"I was helping your friends,"
Ava tells Mia.

"I already know you're a star!"

Ava gives Mia a big hug!
"Will you dance with me?"
Ava asks.

The sisters dance together!

When she grows up
Mia is going to be
just like her big sister—
a dancing star!

Dictionary

Theater

(you say it like this: the-a-ter)

A building where dancers perform

Plié

(you say it like this: plee-ay)

A dance position where you

bend at the knees

Toe Shoes

(you say it like this: tow shooz)

The shoes that ballet dancers wear

Mïa
and the
Tiny Toe Shoes

by Robin Farley
pictures by Aleksey and Olga Ivanov

Today is a big day.
Mia is helping
the littlest dancers.

Today, Mia will teach
them how to dance!

"Class," sings Miss Bird,
"Mia is going to show us
some new dance steps."

Mia smiles at Miss Bird.

She will not let her down.

"Let's start with
first position," says Mia.

Mia puts her heels together.

She moves her toes apart.

The little dancers try to copy her.

Liz bends her knees.
"Try keeping your legs stiff,"
Mia says gently.

Liz wobbles back and forth.
This is hard for her.

"Now we'll try
second position," Mia says.

Mia takes a small step
to one side.

Kate takes a sideways hop.

Her feet are far, far apart.

"Take just a little step,"
says Mia.

She sees Kate frown.

"Last one," Mia says.

"Third position!"

Mia points one toe.
She moves the foot
in front.

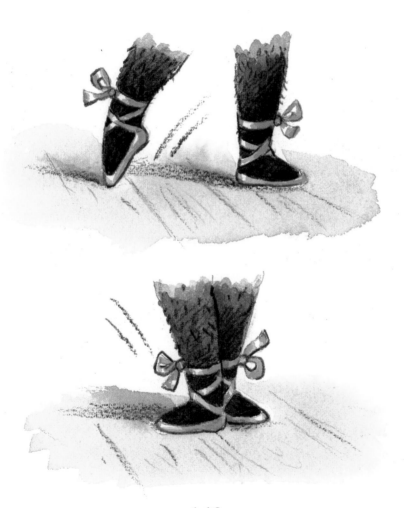

Jane kicks

when she moves her foot.

"Oh my!" says Mia.

"Let's try the steps together,"
Mia tells the class.
She looks around the room.

Liz is wobbling.

Kate is hopping.

Jane is kicking.

"This is not working,"

says Mia.

How will she teach her dance?

Then Mia has an idea.

"These steps are hard," she says,

"but you are good dancers!"

Mia tells the class her plan.
Miss Bird is ready
to watch their dance.

Mia puts on music.

"First position," she calls.

Liz wobbles up front.

"Now, bend!" sings Mia.
Liz turns her wobble
into a fancy bow!

"Second position," Mia says.

Kate starts to move her feet.

"Leap!" Mia tells her.

Kate's big hop

turns into a soaring leap!

"Third position," says Mia.

The girls start to move.

"Kick!" Mia calls to Jane.

Jane kicks her leg up
super high!

"How grand!" Miss Bird cheers.
"You turned the hardest steps
into your best moves!

I'm proud of you all,"
sings Miss Bird.
Miss Bird gives everyone
a big hug.

Dictionary

Wobbling
(you say it like this: wah-bull-ing)
When a ballerina just can't keep her legs still

Leap
(you say it like this: leep)
Taking a big jump

Soaring
(you say it like this: sor-ing)
Leaping through the air

158